BROKEN WATER

BRONTË STONE

Salt of the Earth Press

This is a work of fiction. Names, characters, and incidents are products of the author's imagination or are used fictitiously and are not to be construed as real. Any resemblance to actual organizations or persons, living or dead, is entirely coincidental.

Salt of the Earth Press
W4456 Hwy 63
Springbrook, Wisconsin 54875

Copyright © 2015 by Brontë Stone
ISBN 978-0-9849183-4-8
www. saltpress.com

For my midwife.

NOTES:

The black family living in a shanty at the top of the hill did not actually live in Boulder City until a few years after this story takes place. There were no authorized black personnel or residents of Boulder City in 1932/33. However, Henry and Ocie Bradley, an African American couple, did eventually live there, around 1938, in a house in that location, built from what had originally been a ticket booth for Grand Canyon Airlines. They only lived there for about a year before a fire damaged their house. They built a home on Avenue K and lived there until sometime in the 1940's. I don't know if they had any children while living in Boulder City. Jane and William Crocker in this story are a product of my imagination other than they are black and live in the same place as the Bradleys did.

There is some disagreement over who actually planted the Elm saplings in the parkways along the avenues. The opinion has long been held that the city planners planted them but one story has a "Johnny Appleseed" planting them on his own initiative.

Thank you to those who read this story for historical accuracy. My mistakes and deliberate inventions are my own, and not theirs.

Brontë Stone

Us Old Boys on Boulder Dam

By Claude Rader, a worker on Hoover Dam, 1931

Abe Lincoln freed the negroes
And old Nero he burned Rome,
But the Big Six helped depression
When they gave the stiff a home.
In a nice bunk house their sleepin'
They're workin' every day,
The hungry look has vanished
For they got three squares a day.
You'll find tall Lou from Kal-a-ma-zoo,
And Slim from Alabam,
Mixed in with all the rest of us
Old boys from Boulder Dam.
And the fallin' rocks can't scare us
Nor the scorchin' rays of the sun,
We've rode the rods and brakebeams
Ragged and on the bum.

And they gave us jobs and fed us
When we needed it you bet,
And we all are truly thankful
With no feelings of regret.
So we're stickin' till the finish
There's me and Ike and Sam,
And we're gettin' fat and stakie
Us old boys on Boulder Dam.
There are thousands we know that knock it
And holler that they are cheap,
But to us it brings no worry
Not a moments loss of sleep.
For we've been here since it started,
We're use to all the slam,
And we're stickin' to the finish
Us old boys on Boulder Dam.

CHAPTER ONE
1932 - KANSAS

The wind picked up and pulled soil from the earth. It rushed across the land, gathering more dust as it blew. East. The dust was all blowing East. The small group of people dressed in clothes so old and worn and dusty that they looked gray, stood outside the house, raw wood with not a speck of paint left on its boards, having been sandblasted by the infernal dust storms. A few trees, stripped nearly bare of leaves, at the side of the house, bent in the wind. Other than that, the land was flat and barren and no other houses could be seen, hidden in the dusty air.

Carol and her husband Mac Blair, gave kisses and hugs and got in the car, a 1928 Flivver that had seen better days. The back seat of the Model T was full of their belongings and on the top was a mattress, strapped with rope. They had been married just three months.

"Be sure to write!" an older woman called out as the car slowly pulled away, down the dirt road, away from the dismal farm where nothing grew, heading West, away from the dust, and into the wind. Carol leaned out the window and waved good bye to her mother and figured it was the last she'd see of her family and the only home she'd lived in for twenty years, in fact, the only home she'd ever known . Tears blew back into her ears as she turned forward, and the wind whipped her short brown hair, stinging her face.

"Don't cry, sweetie," Mac said distractedly. "You're going to love Nevada! To hell with farming! I'm going to make so much money working on the Boulder Canyon Project we're going to be rich." On and on his voice went, extolling the virtues of moving hundreds of miles away from their families. Eventually, with no reply from his wife, his voice wound down and the only sound was the wind blowing, incessantly, carrying the prairie back East.

They had lived in Kansas all their lives. Everything they knew was there. Sure, there was a drought right now but Carol was a farmer's daughter; she knew that all it would take was one good year and they would be well off. Corn and wheat would grow again, cows would produce sweet milk and the prairie would bloom like it had when she was a child.

The dry prairie, now reduced to a wasteland of dirt, sped by the open window that Carol looked out of as she thought about her home rapidly disappearing behind her.

When she had married Mac last June, she had supposed, had she given it any thought, that they would live out their lives right there in the same place they'd been born. She'd have babies and grow a garden while Mac would farm. Her mother and father and brothers and sisters would be close by and nothing would change.

But Mac had had different ideas. As soon as he heard about Hoover's big project, a huge dam built out West in a canyon, he was itching to go. Itching to be a part of the biggest dam in the world.

He heard that each worker would get a house, and the wages were very good, especially during a depression. Sure, it was dangerous work but he was young and fearless. Maybe he'd get to be on one of the high wire jobs or a dynamite crew. Wouldn't that be something?

Anything would be better than the Kansas dust storms! He hated eating dirt every day. He wanted more and better for his family and the future was out West. Even without a depression going on, at his age of twenty-one, a job and a house would be a sign of success.

He pushed his hair back from his face and tucked the lank, pale strands behind his ears. His thin face, prematurely haggard from the stress of too little food, too much worry, pinched. Why couldn't Carol be happy and excited, too?

He glanced over at her. She was hunched to the side staring blankly out the window, one hand having gathered the short strands of her hair in a fist to keep it from blowing into her face. He grimaced. It was going to be a long trip.

Carol clenched her teeth against the hopelessness she felt. Didn't Mac understand that she was leaving everything, everyone? Ma had always said a good wife followed her husband, as she herself had done, traveling from the lush farm lands of Ohio to the flat prairie of Kansas, uprooted like a tender plant. Carol wanted to be a good wife but it was so hard to abandon her whole life to follow Mac's dream.

"When I get to Nevada, I'm going to catch me a rattler and you can cook it up. What do you think of that? I hear they taste like chicken."

Carol didn't even respond to his almost continual jabbering. She watched the land as it changed from prairie to desert, huge purple mountains, rugged and stark, looming on the horizon. How tiny and insignificant she felt here in the wide open desert, dwarfed by a landscape where no people settled, no friendly cook stove smoke lazily rose in the distant still air.

"I have to use the facilities," Carol said. She squirmed in discomfort on the hard leather seat of the car.

"Facilities? Hoo boy, that's funny." Mac slapped his thigh in glee. "There's no facilities here. Look." He swept his arm across the vista before them; a valley wide and desolate, greyish-green scrub, and heat waves shimmering above the the asphalt of Route 66. "You see any facilities?" he laughed as he pulled the car over to the side of the road.

Carol got out of the car and stretched. There wasn't even a bush to provide privacy, just some little scrubby creosote brush.

She walked off into the desert a ways but stopped in mortification. There was no way to empty her aching bladder without exposing herself.

"What's keeping you? Do your business so we can get back on the road. I want to make Flagstaff by dark."

"I can't, Mac. There's no place to be private."

"Oh, for God's sake, Carol. There's no one around. Just squat and pee."

Resigned, Carol chose the fullest bush she could find and reached under her dress to pull her drawers down. When she was finished she walked back to the car where Mac stood, staring dreamily at the road ahead. "This is sure some adventure, isn't it?"

Hundreds of other men had the same idea. Every day desperate men applied for a job on the Boulder Canyon Project. Mac was hired more because he was thin and wiry than because he looked strong and capable. His job would be a High Scaler, dangling from lines over the rock walls of the canyon, hundred of feet above the canyon floor and clearing it in preparation for the dynamite crew.

The work was hot and dry and dangerous. But it suited him. He loved hanging from a rope line, bouncing off the rocks. He felt important when he called out directions to the men above. "More line!" he yelled. "Ready!" he called.

While he was hanging over the edge of the canyon lip, Carol was trying to make a home out of what was, essentially, a tent. In an area that overlooked the valley where a lake would form once the dam was completed, many new workers lived in temporary houses until a company house on the Avenues in town became available. Theirs had a frame of sorts and was covered with a tarp. She cooked over a fire and peed in a bucket. She could hear the other women yelling at their children, crying to their men, complaining to their neighbors. The heat was oppressive and when winter came, the wind seemed colder than Kansas since there wasn't anything to stop it from creeping in around the tarp walls and invading the warmth of her bedding.

When payday came around, on the 10th and 25th of each month, Mac always had a reason why he had to go into Las Vegas with his friends, thirty-three miles on the road they called the Widowmaker. When he came home his paycheck was always nearly gone with another couple weeks of pinching pennies and making do ahead. He could always eat at the Commissary where three square meals were available as well as packed lunches, as much as he wanted, too. Because of that, she supposed he didn't understand that she was living off of oatmeal and coffee.

Kansas had prepared her for a life of deprivation. She had left there too thin, her naturally slight body made gaunt from hunger and she hadn't really gained too much weight since.

As she scrubbed dishes in a beat up old metal dishpan, she wondered what had happened to all the big talk about money and a house and a better life. Other women also had dishpans set up on makeshift worktables outside their little tent houses. Laundry flapped on rope strung here and there, children with runny noses and perpetually dirty faces ran helter skelter, and some even went without pants to save on laundry for those who had trouble holding their bladders.

Carol longed for home. She romanticized the prairie and downplayed the drought in her homesickness. The tiny house she grew up in didn't seem so drafty or ramshackle in her imagination.

"Mrs. Blair! Mrs. Blair!" Carol looked up in the direction of the voice calling her name, disturbing her thoughts. Her neighbor was waving a letter in her hand.

CHAPTER TWO

October 12, 1932
Dear Carol,

I am glad to hear Mac found himself a job. That high scaler work sounds hard and frightening but he always was a brave boy and a little bit on the adventurous side so I suppose it suits him.

I have lived in worse places than a tent in the desert so I can't feel too sorry for you. When your Pa and I first came out to the Plains we had plans to build us a cabin but there wasn't any trees to use for lumber. The cost of buying was dear since it had to be shipped out from back East and we had little money to spare. An old timer told us how to build a soddy so that's what we did. I was expecting your big brother Harold so I couldn't help much with the lifting but I sure helped cut them strips of sod. I watched the walls rise and thought it was a mansion after living in the wagon – and under it – for so long. But when the rain came and the bugs hid in the walls, I wasn't too happy. Let me tell you!

Back in them olden days the rains would come and the prairie would bloom. My, how lovely it was. Every color there is as far as the eye could see and the grass so green it hurt your eyes. Seemed your Pa would throw a seed in the ground and up would sprout a crop. Back then we grew a lot of watermelon, not the corn and wheat we been trying to grow these past few years.

It is a different world here from what it was. It hasn't rained in I don't know how long but the winds never stops. Just blows and blows. Some days I think I will go crazy listening to it whistle through the cracks in this old house. And these days the bugs are green worms, tarantulas and black widows. I have to sweep the walls around the beds before we retire at night for fear Molly or Bill will get bit and die in their sleep.

What crops we got to grow is all dried up and dead now. One day the corn looked good and we were counting our eggs before they were hatched. Within a few days it was all dead. But it will make silage for the cattle so your Pa cut it. I do try to look on the bright side but it is hard some days.

The hens are still laying and the cow is still making milk. Every few days I load up what I got and your Pa drives me into town. I usually make about a dollar and we buy some groceries and put 25 cents into the gas tank. That's enough to get home and to return when I have enough to bring to town again.

Harold is going to move to California. He talked with some folks down in No Man's Land. Their kin went and just love it. Everything is green and there's orange groves as far as the eye can see. Work to be had, too! But they did mention that their kin encountered a sign as they came into California that said "Okies Go Home!" Harold figures since he's not an Okie he'll be all right.

I am glad it's working out for you there, daughter. Perhaps if you cut out some pictures from a magazine to hang on the walls it will seem more homey.

We miss you. Please write back.

With love and affection,
Your Ma

The winter had been long and hard in the little tent house but now that Spring was here, the desert was greening up, the sky seemed endlessly blue and Carol felt some hope that she and Mac would be moved into a Six Company house on the Avenues before the heat of summer. She tidied up her space as best she could, shaking the sand tracked in off of several throw rugs padding the rough wood floor.

As a child in Kansas, May Day had been a flower filled celebration. She and her younger sister, Molly had made little posies from the wild flowers growing on the prairie and gave them to their mother. That was before the drought had stolen Ma's happiness. May Day was past and had gone by like every other day, and the days since had crept along with the chaos of living in the tent city. Carol wondered if Molly had remembered the day, and if there were even any wild flowers to give to her mother on the dry and dusty prairie.

Doing the best she could with what she had, Carol combed her hair and using a little spit, tamed a stray curl. She chose a hat, she only had two, and pinned it into place. It was a lovely deep blue felt hat, round with a little netting over the top. It was the tenth, payday, and she liked to make a nice meal for Mac. Having no refrigerator or ice box meant that if she wanted meat she had to go to town to buy it, wrap it in a wet cloth and put it in a shady spot until time to cook dinner. She looked forward to the fragrant scent of a good dinner cooking and the pleasure of watching her husband enjoy the meal.

Outside the sun was already hot, and she squinted against the bright sky. It took a moment for her eyes to adjust, and she took the time to take a deep breath of the clear air. "Hello there, Mrs. McGraff!" she called out to a lady living a few houses down.

"Hello, Mrs. Blair! Are you going into town? Could you pick me up some coffee?"

Carol tucked Mrs. McGraff's quarter in her pocketbook and walked briskly up the hill toward Boulder City proper.

The walk into town to the store was across the railroad tracks, busy with carrying huge crates and giant pieces of machinery. Up the hill and past the Water Treatment Plant, then by the engineers' homes, bungalows built in a Mediterranean style with green lawns and staked saplings, and across the highway, where all the big trucks rushed past on the way to and from the dam. Uptown was up-hill from just about everything in Boulder City and Carol walked it at least every other day to buy groceries.

She stopped by the Post Office and found a letter from Ma. Smiling she slit the top with her fingernail and stopped right there on the concrete sidewalk to read the onion skin thin paper sheets cramped with her mother's writing.

CHAPTER THREE

April 23, 1933

Dear Carol,

I am so glad you are there and not suffering like we been here in Kansas. How long do you think before you and Mac will get one of those houses for the workers? You say the water will be piped right into the house? I can't hardly even imagine such a thing.

Pa took Bill with him to plow and no sooner did they get the field done than a duster rolled in and took the field away. Just blew the ground off into the sky. The cows bawl something terrible when that dust kicks up. It can choke them and make them go blind so Pa tries to bring them into the barn if the wind blows too much sand. Afterward the air is black and heavy and what little grass we have is covered up. The tumbleweeds that collect on the barb wire fences are being used for cattle feed on some folks' places.

It's just steady wind. I've never seen it so bad as it's been these past 2 months. The wheat what came up, got buried and shriveled dead.

I wake in the morning and I think it's hopeless. The prairie will never come back. My children are scattering and soon it will be only me and Pa here in this house surrounded by sand.

President Roosevelt has a New Deal to help out folks who are hurting. Did you hear about it out there in the West? I asked Harold to sign up for the CCC but he was bound and determined to head out to California. He left a week ago Saturday, right before Easter Sunday and I cried a few tears to see him go. I suppose it's always sad when the first born child leaves the nest.

A few boys from around these parts have signed up for the CCC. I hear they're going to plant a forest to try and stop these infernal dust storms. They will earn $30 a month and $25 of that will go *back to their families. Can you imagine what $25 a month would do to help out around here? But Harold wanted to go West. He reminded me he's almost 25 and it's time he made his way in the world. I think you getting married and then leaving made him think about getting married, settling down and all that.*

I hope he writes. I have this feeling he drove off into the sunset and I'll never hear from him again. A mother's heart is a funny thing!

We miss you. Please write back.

With love and affection,
Your Ma

arol's heart sank at reading how her family was suffering. That selfish Harold, running off to California when her parents needed him. Of course, she had left them, too and followed her husband but that was different so she felt no guilt. However, as the oldest son, Harold should have stayed. She carefully folded the paper and tucked the sheets back into the envelope and then into her bag.

The grocery store was across a small park from the post office and it was a pleasure to linger in the grassy spot. Carol wished she could slip her shoes off and feel the grass on her feet. Even the little trees gave a welcome shade.

On paydays the town was usually pretty busy. Men who got off shift earlier in the day had already received their paychecks and they were stocking up at the store or splurging on a piece of pie at the diner, or watching a movie at the air con-ditioned theater. Others, who worked the day shift, were not yet home but their wives shopped for a special dinner, an air of excitement Uptown be-cause the men would be home soon with money in their pockets. Carol nodded a greeting to a few fa-miliar faces, and then headed home. Walking back was just as hard, even though it was almost entirely downhill, because she was carrying her purchases in bags she'd crocheted from cotton string.

Carol shifted the string bags from hand to hand, finger to finger, the thin crocheted handle cutting into her skin. Mac would be home by the time she got there and she hoped they would have a calm evening. She had a good dinner planned with the ingredients she was carrying. As she crossed the railroad tracks she saw a commotion at her place, a big, official looking car parked there and the women of the neighborhood gathered around. They saw her coming and grew silent, watching her approach.

When she was about 50 yards away a man came forward, hat in hand, his white linen suit jacket and loose pants legs flapping slightly in the breeze. "Mrs. Blair," he said, "I am sorry to inform you that there's been an accident." Carol's heart skipped a beat. An accident? Dynamite? A fall to the canyon floor? How many ways there were for Mac to hurt himself at his job. She was mute, struck dumb by her imagination carrying her thoughts in all the directions possible,

"Mr. Blair was traveling in a car on the road to Las Vegas when he lost control."

"The road to Las Vegas?" she repeated. In her head she thought, "Damn him! He was going to spend his paycheck. Maybe this will cure him of being irresponsible."

"I'm sorry, Ma'am. He died instantly."

As the words impacted her brain, her fingers released the crocheted bags of groceries and they dropped to the dusty ground and her purchases, the groceries that would have made Mac a nice supper, rolled about her feet. That action galvanized the crowd and they rushed forward, clucking over her, patting her shoulders, stroking her arms.

"You can stay on in your home until the end of the month but then it will have to be vacated for another worker." The important man in his fancy suit drove away in his big car and left Carol standing there next to the little tent house.

Looking up, she saw Mrs. McGraff's anxious face and she bent over to retrieve the small bag of coffee beans she'd picked up for her. Thrusting it into her neighbor's hands, Carol said, "I didn't forget your coffee."

CHAPTER FOUR

As the sun rose over the Colorado River valley, where a lake would form after the completion of Boulder Dam, Carol sat clutching a shawl around her shoulder against the cool May morning. The tents and shacks of her neighbors were dark and quiet now, their excitement at the unexpected tragedy of the day before forgotten.

Mac had been driving their car, which Carol noticed was missing as soon as the crowd had cleared the day before. They didn't have much but that car would have gotten her home to Kansas. He'd cashed his paycheck before leaving town and it was assumed that the money had burned or blown away in the wreck. There she was, penniless, and soon to be homeless.

She took stock of her belongings and as the day proceeded, the women of the neighborhood came like vultures to relieve her of as much as they could. Mac's clothes went. Her wedding dress, rolled up in muslin and wrapped in tissue paper, was carried off under the arm of a woman from the next street. Her books were picked over and disappeared. Dishes, pots, pans, linens, all taken away by sympathetic women, foreheads crinkled and mouths down turned as they left Carol's tent with arms full. She rolled her clothes up as tightly as she could and tucked them into her string grocery bags. What didn't fit, she would leave behind.

The Federal Government ran Boulder City under the direction of Sims Ely. It was a closed community, built for the men who would be working on Boulder Dam, and families were merely tolerated. There were very few jobs for women, no real opportunity to earn some money with which to leave. She didn't want to wait around for the new people to arrive, ready to move into her tent house, but she had no where to go. She decided to ask at

the Six Company office, the company that held the
contract to build the dam and was the employer of
almost everyone in town, if they could loan her the
money for rail fare back to Kansas. If that failed,
she'd go to Mr. Ely himself.

She left the shack for the last time, her bags
looped over her fingers, a handbag swinging from
her wrist, and began the walk uptown.

Coming off a twelve-hour shift on the project down in the canyon, Tim reminded himself that
he was fortunate he had a car and could go home
when he was done, instead of having to wait for Big
Bertha, one of the canvas walled double-decker
trucks that carried men to and from the job site.
He stood from his drafting table and stretched his
back, hearing the vertebra crackle from disuse.
Even though he'd put in more hours than he cared
to think about, there was one last detail he needed
to finalize and unfortunately the file he needed to

finish was at home. The eight miles up to Boulder City seemed like a thousand miles as he wearily shut off the drafting light over his table and made his way out of the barracks-like building to his car.

He was only one of many engineers working on the project and a neighborhood had been set aside for them. The houses were brick or stucco and lawns were laid, trees planted, on one of the highest points in town. Tim's house would soon be finished but in the meantime he was living in a Six Company house, one of the very small homes built for workers and their families, in the Avenues. Avenue C, where he was staying, was lined with identical houses.

The houses were boxes thrown together on the desert floor, most were just three rooms and a screened porch, sided in ship lap with interiors clad in the thinnest gypsum board available. At some of the places the inhabitants had made an effort to plant grass and the Administration had planted thousands of Elm trees between the sidewalks and streets. The cottages had all been painted white but some had window trim or doors painted a different color by the workers and their families: green, brown, black. If you looked closely, you would see the differences but just a glance conveyed complete and utter conformity. Avenue after avenue was lined with the exact same house, duplicated in the hundreds.

Children played in the streets, since there were so few cars. Laundry flapped on lines strung across back yards. Women shared recipes and stories of marital discord over coffee sipped while sitting on the concrete stoops in front of each identical door. And over it all the Federal Government kept control, holding a tight reign. No drinking and no gambling, unlike Las Vegas just over the hill and down in the next valley where speakeasies and wild behavior were the norm. A strict mode of behavior and a curfew were enforced in Boulder City. Under other circumstances, the citizens might have objected but there was little discord. They were so thankful to have jobs while the rest of the country suffered the depression. The houses were tiny but they had running water and electricity and a brand new elementary school was being built uptown.

As Tim turned down Avenue C he saw a woman walking, carrying two bulging strings bags. She wasn't very tall and her slight frame made her look even smaller, fragile and vulnerable. Her short brown hair was neatly combed and tucked behind her ears, and a small blue hat was balanced on her head, though it looked like it might have slipped a little to one side. Her dress was clean, though faded; a flowery print he thought. He pulled into his driveway just as she reached the edge of his yard and her eyes briefly met his. "Hello," he said simply for lack of a better response.

Carol nodded in reply, shifting the bags from finger to finger, hitching her shoulder up to prevent her purse from sliding further down her arm.

"Your bags look heavy. Can I help you carry them somewhere?"

"No, thank you." She paused and looked up at the sky and he saw that she had been crying. "I don't really know where I'm going."

At a loss, Tim stood there by his car in the driveway while Carol stood on the sidewalk. Finally he made a decision. "You look like you need a break. Can I offer you some iced tea"

The tiny house was neat, mainly because there were so few furnishings, and no decorations. Freshly painted white walls, speckled linoleum covering the floors, plain draperies, cream with a pale green fern pattern, hung on the windows, it felt more like a hotel than someone's home. That brought to mind all of her belongings she'd had to get rid of just that morning and she began to cry again.

Tim turned from the open refrigerator with a glass pitcher of iced tea. "Now, now," he said awkwardly, patting her shoulder. "Put down those bags, drink this tea, and tell me what seems to be the trouble." He filled two glasses with ice cubes from the built in freezer and then poured the tea over, causing it to crackle and pop.

After a long drink of the cold tea, Carol looked around her and wondered how she had ended up in this situation. She was a farmer's daughter from Kansas, not some pioneer with wanderlust! That had been Mac, always wanting something new, something better, something else.

"My husband worked on the dam," she said. "Yesterday he died."

The story she told, unfortunately, sounded all too familiar. Tim had seen variations of it a few times since arriving at the Boulder Canyon Project. Men who had been living without enough work, or food, or comfort, suffering through the effects

of the depression for years, suddenly found themselves with cash every payday, plates heaped with
nourishing food at the commissary each meal, beds
inside houses inside a town, and simply couldn't
handle it. After all the deprivation they went a little crazy and ate too much and spent their money
on liquor and gambling and some of them lost the
very jobs that had been their salvation. Thankfully,
fewer yet lost their lives.

"Where were you going just now?" Tim
asked.

"I had thought to ask the company to loan
me train fare back to Kansas but they said they
couldn't. My next plan was to talk to Mr. Ely," Carol said as she wiped her cheeks with the back of her
hand.

Tim gasped. Was the woman mad? Sims Ely
was a hard nosed, mean, tyrant. He'd toss this poor
woman out at the gates and wouldn't care what became of her. Thank goodness Tim had run across
her path.

"Listen," he paused and ran his hand over
his face stalling for a solution. "You can't ask Mr.
Ely for help. Trust me, you just can't. But I'm not
sure what you should do right now, and I have to go

back to work; I only came home to get a file I need. You can stay here and when I get home we can figure out some solution to your problem."

Tim showed Carol the little porch room off the living room. A day bed was set up there for hot nights where a person could catch a breeze through the screened windows. Hot weather hadn't started for the year and it wouldn't be too bad to rest in.

Soon he was gone, his car disappearing up the street. Carol decided she would find some way to repay him for his kindness and a quick look around determined that laundry needed to be done and a wringer washer on the enclosed back porch would make quick work of it.

She really couldn't get over the water. Most houses didn't have lawns because the City Management didn't want water wasted but the drain water from washing was often used to irrigate a garden or small patch of grass. If there was one thing she knew, it was how to conserve water for maximum benefit after living through drought in Kansas and the rough situation in her little tent house. She wasn't surprised that as she was washing, a plump woman showed up at the back door with a bucket.

"Hi there." Her blonde hair was pulled back

in a ponytail and she wore glasses. She introduced herself as Mary Keith, a neighbor, and made an immediate assumption that Carol was Tim's wife. "We've been wondering when Mr. Marshal's family was going to arrive."

Carol didn't say much. She didn't want to get Tim in trouble for letting her stay there and she didn't want to get thrown off the town site.

"Do you mind if I have some of your wash water? I have a little garden started over yonder," she pointed to the sandy lot next door.

"What do you have planted?"

Before long the two were discussing the merits of various vegetables and Mary offered to share some seeds.

It wasn't that Carol believed that she was Tim's wife, or even deliberately wanted to perpetuate the assumption, but rather that she got caught up in the moment. With Mary's help, Carol was soon digging a little garden plot by the back door and another, for flowers, by the front door.

She found herself humming along to the radio while she swept the desert sand from the kitchen floor, washed dishes, made beds and folded the now dry laundry. The news broadcast kept her company while she made dinner and then, when Tim didn't show up, went to bed in the little porch room off the living room to the sound of President Roosevelt's fireside chat.

CHAPTER FIVE

The logistics of the Boulder Canyon Project were complicated and Tim's work as one of the many engineers was to painstakingly plan every part of the job before it occurred. The office was crowded with desks, drafting tables and men in a constantly shifting dance. He had worked through the night after an unexpected snag required a new approach and then through the next day he made sure the new plan was implemented, and worked. The pressure to come in under budget and ahead of time was felt by everyone in the canyon and to a man, they toiled at making it happen.

He noticed the trucks were leaving for

town, filled with the day shift workers, and looked around himself. The new plans were good and the trouble had been averted. The other engineers had moved on to more pressing concerns or had left for the day. With a groan, Tim stood and stretched out the kink in his back. His tie, long loosened from his neck, hung limply and he held his suit jacket by a finger over his shoulder as he made his way to his car.

The streets of Boulder City were dark and quiet, since only authorized and necessary people were allowed to be about at night after curfew. Tim peeled his suit off and flopped down on his bed to fall almost instantly asleep. His last thoughts were of the rail trip he had to make to the offices of the Southern California Edison Electric Company in Los Angeles.

The smell of coffee, bacon and toast worked its way into his dream and it took a minute for him to realize that it was real, when he finally opened his eyes. He lay there for a moment until he decided it must be coming from the next house down the street. As he rose he noticed his bedroom door was pulled almost completely shut and he paused, trying to remember the night before when he came home. Why would he have closed it?

Carol looked up just as Tim stepped around the doorway from the bedroom. She was standing at the electric range, turning crisply browning bacon and smiled brightly at his surprised face. When the surprise didn't fade her heart began pounding in her chest in fear. Would he send her away? She looked back at the pan on the stove, her vision blurring with tears. All this food, the water pouring from the pipes enabling her to start her little garden, the neighbors just right next door, all of this was like heaven after her years of deprivation in the drought and depression in Kansas.

She realized she'd been in dreamland. This wasn't her home, or her yard. Those weren't her neighbors waking up in the houses on either side with the smells of their breakfasts cooking mingling with hers. Her husband was dead, ready to be buried in the cemetery outside of town and strangers had hauled away her entire life's worth of memories in the form of books and pictures and mementos. This man was going to make her leave. She saw it in his surprised face and realized that as much as she had wanted to go home, go back to the familiar way of life on the prairie, in reality she didn't want to leave. She wanted the security of food, and shelter and a future that included watching tomatoes ripen.

Slowly she turned the burner off and wiped her hands on the makeshift apron around her waist, a dishtowel pinned at her back.

"I'm sorry. I presumed too much. I'll be out of your hair in a jiffy." She spoke quietly as she reached back and unpinned the towel.

Tim was shocked because he'd forgotten all about the woman he'd rescued. As memory came back of her desolation and hopelessness, he schooled his face to a calm expression.

"Smells good," he said cheerfully as he reached by her to snag a piece of bacon. "I have to get back to work. Just make yourself at home and when I get back we'll talk."

She was in the same spot when he came back to the kitchen awhile later. He had washed the two days of anxious work sweat from his body and dressed in a fresh suit, his hair wetly combed back from his forehead. "I have to travel to Los Angeles today and won't be back for a couple of days, at least. I'll see you then." In a moment of compassion he reached out and squeezed her arm as he passed her on the way to the back door.

His mind was already shifting to the tasks ahead of him for the day as he closed the porch door. Something was different and he stopped to look around. A board lay at the bottom of the steps and off to the left was a garden plot, tilled and rich with soil, not the sand of the desert. A bucket nearby indicated how she must be watering it. He leaned closer and saw that nothing was growing yet, but if the markers at the end of each row were any indication there would be carrots, radishes, tomatoes and lettuce.

Tim remembered how, as a child, there had always been a garden off the kitchen door. One of his earliest memories was of his mother, hair in a kerchief, weeding while he played nearby in the mud. He must have been three or four. He took a deep breath of the desert morning full of the scent of creosote bush and fresh air. With no time for woolgathering, he went directly to the car and headed out.

CHAPTER SIX

The little garden was growing. Each day Carol filled a bucket with water from the spigot by the back door, or the washing machine, or even the dish water, and poured it around the rows. Tomatoes, cucumbers, squash and peas along with the usual salad things were reaching tiny green points through the soil towards the sun. The soil was dark and rich from the manure her neighbor brought her, collected from the edge of the park the Feds were building up the hill. In reward, sprouts were curling up out of the dark, damp ground, green and healthy.

Such a simple thing, she thought and she carried the bucket around to the front flower bed:

water and growing a garden. If only her mother could see it, my how she'd be impressed. Carol could remember back in the 20's when she was a little girl and Kansas was a green, growing place. But when she'd left there, it was sand with fierce winds that blew and sucked the breath out of your lungs. To grow anything required a herculean effort but here she was, unlimited water from a pipe in the ground, making a little oasis in the desert.

Tim had come back from his trip to California a week or so ago and hadn't said a word about her leaving, so she kept her mouth shut. While he was gone, Mac's funeral had been held, presided over by a minister, and attended by a few Six Company men, all strangers to her. She had walked the mile or so out to the graveyard and no one had asked where she was staying or what her plans were. When it was over, she'd walked back, and no one had offered her a ride.

Dribbling water over the flower seedlings sprouting near the front steps, she pondered how she might be invisible for all the attention anyone paid to her. Some days she didn't speak a word to anyone and had to test out her voice just to see if it still worked. If she saw Tim at all it was briefly as he left in the morning since he usually came home late in the night after she was in bed. She would say "good morning" to which he would respond in kind with a smile. She always left him a plate of supper in the refrigerator and in the morning he might comment on it. "Good meat loaf last night. Thanks."

She had just straightened up when she saw the neighbor lady rush out of her house, a baby on her hip. The child was about nine months old and had a runny nose and from the looks of it, a dirty diaper, sagging down his thin legs. "Carol!" the woman called to her.

"Hello, Mary," Carol said. "Where are you off to in such a rush?"

"Margaret Wood is having pains! Her last baby came fast and she doesn't think she can make it to Las Vegas!"

Carol shuddered. The thirty-three mile trip into Las Vegas to a hospital was bad enough, but to do it in labor sounded awful. The hospital built at the top of Uptown was for workers and as yet no woman had been admitted for a delivery.

Back home, Carol's mother had often helped neighbor ladies out when their time had come and sometimes Carol came along to tend older children. "Can I help?" she asked.

"Do you have any experience with birthing?"

"Some. A little." She thought about those births she'd attended, fetching a wet cloth to cool a forhead, holding a glass of water for a woman to take a long drink, rubbing a lower back tight with anxiety.

Mary shifted her baby to the other hip. "Would you mind going to her? Bobby is sick, teething I think. She just lives at 646."

Carol set the bucket down and briskly walked down the street to the Woods' house. It was a little Six Company shack, one up from the corner and no effort had been made to plant anything. Just sand surrounded the small house. The Woods hadn't been there long and she knew they had arrived in a car with little else but their four children.

At her tap on the door, a girl of about five answered. "Ma's in there," she said and pointed back toward the bedroom.

Carol could hear her groans, the deep guttural sounds of a woman beginning to push. She didn't bother to knock, just opened the door and found Margaret laying on her bed, curled up on her side, panting. Her face glistened with sweat and her dress was twisted around her.

Margaret opened her eyes and saw Carol in her doorway. "I tried to wait. My husband is working and I really tried to wait but I just can't." Her voice trailed off and her eyes lost focus as another contraction besieged her.

Carol forgot her nerves and quickly pulled the woman's dress up. The baby was already crowning.

"Mrs. Wood... Margaret, try to relax. Your baby is going to be here in just a minute. There's no use fighting it."

Margaret's body pushed once more and the baby's head was born. Carol knew from watching her mother that she should feel for a cord around its neck. Feeling nothing but a fat crease she pulled her hands back. "You're doing fine, Margaret. Just fine."

With the next push the baby slid out and Carol quickly put her hands under its body to receive it. Another girl, she noticed and brought her up to Margaret's chest as the child took a deep breath and cried.

Mother and baby were tucked up in the bed now, with clean bedding. Carol had run the soiled sheets and thin blanket through the ringer washer and hung them out on the line. With the arid desert breeze they would be dry in no time.

Other women from the street had come by with food and good wishes and curiosity. They had oohed and ahhed and cooed over the baby, named Grace. Margaret had joked that she would call her Lickety Split but good sense prevailed.

The older children had crowded around and admired the new sibling and were now playing some game in the front yard that required robust shouts and occasional arguments.

The two-step stomp of a man clearing his feet of sand and stickers sounded on the back porch. The clatter of his metal lunch box hitting the counter came next. The men came home from the Dam site in a double-decker truck called Big Bertha. The sides were open with canvas that could be pulled down to protect them from wind, the rare rain and road debris. Let out at the top of each street, they walked down hill to their homes. "Mr. Wood," Carol greeted him.

As he stood over his wife's bed all he felt was

thankful. A trip to the hospital would have meant lost wages and the doctor's bill. As Carol left he pulled several dollars from his wallet and handed them to her. "It's not much but it's all I can afford. Thank you!"

Carol walked slowly back up the street to Tim's house. She couldn't wait to write her mother and tell her about this recent event. And she had even earned money! Her fist curled tighter around the six folded dollars.

When Tim walked up to the back door after work, the first thing he noticed was a full bucket of water next to Carol's little garden. Inside the house there was no delicious aroma of dinner cooking. For a moment he thought perhaps she'd left. Got on a train and headed back to Kansas. He was surprised at the pain of loss he felt. As he stood in the center of the kitchen looking around he heard a noise at the front door.

A young boy, ten or twelve, stood on the concrete stoop clutching a note. As Tim answered the door, the boy thrust the note out and said, "Here!" On the outside of the note was penned "Midwife."

Tim really didn't have time to let his confusion develop because almost immediately Carol came in the door. Her hair was messy and her dress had a wet spot down the front. "You won't believe what happened to me today!" she exclaimed happily. But before she could go on, Tim handed her the note with a question in his eyes.

"Oh!" she said. And then, upon reading the message inside, said, "I have to go out and help another lady have her baby! I'll explain when I get back! There's a casserole in the refrigerator and fresh lemonade, too."

Those were more words than he had heard the woman speak in the weeks she'd been in his house. He stared at the front door she'd slammed shut behind her as she rushed out.

CHAPTER SEVEN

Leaning back in the wooden chair at the small table in the kitchen, Tim enjoyed a moment of utter contentment. His work was going well and he had impressed the people down in LA at the electric company. When he got home each evening there was good food waiting for him and a cooling breeze was coming in through the windows to make the early summer evening not quite so hot. He gulped down the last swallow of lemonade in his glass just as the front door opened.

She was tired. He could see it in the slope of her shoulders, her short brown hair, damp with sweat, was pushed back from her forehead and her mouth was pinched. As soon as she saw him sitting there, her face lit up and she smiled.

"What's the big mystery that's got you looking like the cat that ate the canary?" he said as he stood, hands full of his dirty dishes.

Carol laughed and hurried to take the dishes from him. "I helped two ladies have their babies today!"

"You're a midwife?" Tim grabbed a dish rag and wiped off the table as Carol set his dinner dishes in the sink.

"No, not really." She smiled again, that satisfied look erasing the fatigue from her face. "Well, I guess I am. Now." Just thinking those thoughts brought a rippling feeling of pleasure through Carol's belly and chest until it had to erupt as a little laugh.

"Let's sit out back and catch the breeze while you tell me all about it." Tim opened the back door and held it while motioning to her with his hand.

They sat on the concrete steps, the sun fading behind the house across the alley. The little garden wasn't yet full of proper plants, but that little spot smelled like good damp, fertile earth.

Carol began by telling about her morning.

Half of what she said didn't register in his mind but her happiness was a pleasure after the worry and hopelessness he had seen on her face when he first met her.

Carol was careful to not tell Tim anything that would embarrass the women she'd helped that day. She spoke of how cute the babies were, the excitement of the older children, and her great sense of satisfaction in being able to be a help. "While I was there, at the last birth, another neighbor came over and asked if I could come to her when her time came. She's not due for another month so I told her I would think about it and give her my answer later. Would you mind? I made a few dollars today and if I can stay for another month I'll have enough to go back to Kansas."

He could have given her the money for train fare. He could afford it. If she refused the charity, he could ask around, find another place for her to stay while she waited on the next birth. Yes, he knew there were other options but he found he was agreeing to her staying with him without voicing those other solutions. He rather liked dinner waiting and fresh lemonade and seeing her little garden. He was enjoying listening to her tell about her day, and knowing she would be there when he woke in the morning.

Until that moment, Tim hadn't realized he was lonely. He was surrounded by people all day, and sometimes all night. The thin walls of the Six Company houses allowed the sounds of families to carry to him. How could he be lonely while constantly in the presence of all that humanity? But as Carol spoke, giggled in pleasure, jumped to fill his glass with more lemonade, he knew that this moment was so much more because she was talking to him, and looking at him, and somehow that was deeply satisfying.

"Sure, you can stay." He tried to sound nonchalant but he felt a surge of pleasure, knowing that she would be there for a while longer.

"All I've been talking about is me! Goodness. How was your day?"

Tim grew excited talking about his work on the historic project and Carol watched as he forgot to be his usual reticent self. His face lit with enthusiasm and his strong arms waved, demonstrating the power of the Colorado River meeting the concrete that would soon be poured to create the dam.

"We're designing huge steel tunnels that

will travel under the rock of the canyon walls . They have to withstand the tremendous force of the river as it's diverted around the riverbed." He took a long drink of tea, ice cubes tinkling against the glass. His Adam's apple moved as he swallowed and Carol was transfixed by his health and vitality.

"Your job is to do all the arithmetic, to figure that out?"

"The equations, yes. But all of the engineers are working on it."

She wanted him to keep talking forever. She wanted this night, rich with the aroma of the living desert, to continue on. She was fascinated by his intellect and dazzled by the importance of his work.

He took another drink and tipped the glass in her direction. Tell me about being a midwife. I've never known one before."

I don't know what a real midwife does." She laughed self-consciously.

"Come on! You're a real midwife. What do you do?"

"Mostly I sit quietly and watch. At first I didn't know what to do with myself. Now, I'm trying to trust that a woman's body knows how to have a baby. I..." she paused, looking for a word.

Her slim knees were touching, the faded flowery fabric of her dress tucked modestly around her thighs where she sat on the step.

"... I suggest," she finished.

"What sort of suggestions?"

Embarrassed by the intimate nature of her work she was silent. Tim could hear her breathing, imagine her mind whirring over what to say. "sometimes it's best if a lady change positions. Sometimes I encourage her to stand up if she's laying down, kneel if she's sitting, or even sit on the commode."

She looked off into the darkness of the back yard, toward the alley where the light of the street lamp on Avenue B made a ray of lighter sand across the sandy strip. The kitchen window fought the gloom with a glow of it's own, and her face was illuminated; her expression spoke of passion, hope, fear, and ultimately courage.

"I just make suggestions and the lady does the work." Her fingers plucked at the fabric over her knees, drawing his eyes down, over her body, along her slim calves, ending at her bare toes buried in the sand at the bottom of the steps.

Later, sitting on the edge of the single bed in the porch room, Carol brushed her hair. Thank goodness Tim had agreed to letting her stay. Being a midwife was the most exciting thing that had ever happened to her and she wasn't quite ready to let it go.

Before long, word of Carol's willingness to attend women got around. Tim got used to coming home and finding her there, tending her little garden, dinner on the table, or the house quiet with a note on the table telling him she'd gone to Avenue D or California Street, which meant she was attending a birth.

There didn't seem to be a right time to tell her to leave. He was enjoying her company too much, though he told himself his reticence was because she was making money for her move home. So far, no one had made an issue of it but as the time came closer to when his house would be ready on the hill, Tim knew he would have to address it.

Carol was an unmarried woman living in a Federal Reservation and that was against the rules.

Sometimes, Carol coming in from a birth, woke him in the night with her tentative movement and muffled noises and he would come out. She was always a little wired and made herself some tea to wind down. She'd tell him a little bit about the family, but was always careful to be respectful to the privacy of the women she served.

Most interesting to her were the Mormon women. The Boulder City group had recently moved a building from Las Vegas to Uptown for their chapel. Carol had attended the open house, as had many on the Avenues, and during that social she was passed around excitedly from one woman to another as "the midwife." If the size of their families were any indication, Carol could imagine them keeping her very busy.

CHAPTER EIGHT

May 30, 1933

Dear Carol,

     *Oh, our hearts are heavy to hear that Mac
has passed. You say it was a car crash. I don't understand why he was driving into Las Vegas. It sounds
like that place is not somewhere a body would want
to go. Gambling and spirits and loose women. My
heart pounds just to hear of it! I've heard it said that
ending Prohibition would put an end to Speakeasies
and Bootlggers but I don't think Kansas will ever go
for that.*

But daughter, you say you couldn't stay in your little tent house and have gone to stay with a friend. What a good person she must be to let you stay there. Make yourself useful and help out as much as you can. If we had the money to buy you a ticket we would surely send for you but maybe some kind soul will let you travel back home with them.

Your friend's house sounds wonderful. Electricity, running water, and even a wireless radio!

We had some excitement here last week. A twister touched down outside of town. Though we weren't directly hit we lost the chicken coop. What chickens that weren't blown away, ran away. The loss of my egg money will be missed.

The kitchen garden was coming up so nicely but the twister tore up the sand and buried my plants and I am afraid it is all lost. Molly has taken a job teaching in the country school house. She will start in the fall. They can't pay her cash money but will give her script which can be used at the store in town for groceries. It can't be helped. The loss of the chickens and the garden have caused much grief. Now we just have to survive until September. It's too bad that she will have to give up her dream of going to the Women's College down there in Chickasha,

Oklahoma but tough times call for tough choices.

It is so blasted hot! I dream of wading in a pond as I did when I was a girl in Ohio. The grit collects on the skin and makes us all itch. What we wouldn't give to be able to take a bath.

The Douglas family in Liberal have been fortunate to have a son who joined up with the CCC. You remember Stan Douglas. Well he is stationed up north of here and his first pay has made all the difference to their family. He is planting trees and writes that it is hard work but the food is good. I saw his ma in the grocery store buying canned goods and fresh meat. I would have liked it if Harold had joined up but he was determined to go to California.

I got a letter from Harold the other day. He tells of eating fresh oranges and seeing the Pacific Ocean. He is working at a garage repairing automobiles and hopes to save up enough money to help us out some. Pa says don't hold your breath but I will because I want to believe that my son has a good and generous heart. And if I don't hold out hope that he will help there is nothing to be hopeful about.

I think the Prairie is done. Pa says this is just a drouth cycle and any day it will start raining but FDR's man, name of Bennet came to town and spoke to a group of farmers. He's a farmer himself and talks smart so all the men listening just ate up his words. He said we might be able to undo what man has done to this prairie. Pa said he didn't like that because it made it sound like the drought and the dust storms were all the farmers' fault. Pa says the man is a crank but folks sure seemed to like him and his regular ways.

    My poor widow daughter, I will say a prayer for you and one of thankfulness for your kind friend who is letting you stay with her.

    Please write back and let us know how you are doing.

With love,

Your Mother

The heat was like a living thing. At dawn it was 90 and by noon over 100. Carol was thankful she didn't have to go to the dam. Tim had told her how it got over 120 in the canyon and though his office was cooled, he wasn't always inside.

She kept a wet towel around her neck and fans blowing on her to keep her cool while she worked around the house. In the afternoon, when the sun beat down on the kitchen window and the sand of the alley behind the house shimmered with heat waves, she turned on the radio and listened to the Betty and Bob show, with all the accompanied drama and love affairs.

It was almost like she had an internal alarm clock, she thought, since she always knew it was time to start dinner and Tim would be home soon.

After the evening they had sat outside and talked he started showing up at dinner time. He said that a big design problem had kept him at work but Carol thought maybe he had been avoiding her.

Sure enough, the sound of the car pulling

into the driveway alerted her to Tim's arrival. She set the last dish on the table and wiped the back of her hand over her glistening forehead just as the porch door opened.

"That smells delicious!" His tie was loose around his neck, his white shirt sleeves rolled up and limp. He opened the refrigerator and pulled out a glass pitcher of iced tea.

"How was your day?" Carol asked as she took two glasses down from the cupboard.

"Hot and long. One of the new men collapsed today. He had come straight from some little town back East, and hadn't had a decent meal in months, maybe years. He saw all the cafeteria food and chowed down. When the whistle blew and he went back out in the sun he just crumpled."

Carol's face pinched in sympathy as she walked to the radio and flipped the toggle switch to off. "Is he all right?"

"Sure. He rested awhile and was back at his job within an hour"

"Mac was like that when we first got here." At Tim's questioning look, she continued. "Kansas had been hard hit with the depression and drought and food was in short supply. It still is. When Mac started work in the canyon he went a little crazy the first time he saw all the food. He got sick, threw it all back up."

"How about you?"

"Me what? Was I hungry? No. I made do. And I didn't have to work like a dog dangling from a leash like the high scalers do. Truth be told, it was hard for me to give myself permission to eat. I kept wanting to save our food for when things got hard again."

Tim dished himself up a big helping of casserole and imagined being that fearful. "I thought you lived on a farm. I have always figured that there would be plenty of surplus food for the farm family."

Carol smiled. "Maybe once upon a time but during the drought we were lucky to keep our kitchen garden alive. Some years, we didn't. I knew people who slaughtered their horses and ate them but thankfully, we didn't have to do that."

They ate in silence for a few moments. "Why do you want to go back there? It sounds," he paused, searching for a word that wouldn't offend her. "It sounds hard."

"I guess I wanted to go back because I have

no place else to go. I don't really have any job skills. And, even as hard as it was, it's home. It's where my people are. "

"You have job skills now!" he said as he saluted her with his glass of lemonade. "You're a midwife!"

She laughed and clinked her glass to his. "How about you? Were you hungry when you got here?"

"No," he shook his head. "My family did better than most. My father owned a firm in New York that built apartments and factories and hospitals, most on speculation. But he was smart, or just didn't trust banks, and put aside some cash. When the stock market crashed he lost the business but the cash kept our family going. Still is. My parents live in the same house I grew up in, my mother has a garden in the same place she always has had, and my father spends his days tinkering around the place."

"But what about you?" He hadn't mentioned himself.

"I'd gotten my engineering degree and went to work for my father just a couple of years before that. When the business folded, I moved back home. I couldn't find a job so when I heard about this project my father wrote an old friend who pulled some strings and got me at the top of the list."

Tim had never gone hungry, Carol marveled. He'd never known hot, dusty winds that buried everything in sand, nor the horror of watching your friends and family fade away before your eyes. "Was everyone back there in New York the same? A garden and money set aside?"

"God, no!" he said as he wiped his mouth and rose to help put the leftovers away. "In the city there's no place to grow a garden, even if you wanted to. I don't know why people always rush to cities when there's a crisis. My parents live outside of town and life was harder but not too much different for us. I lived in the city when I was working for my father and for a little while after the crash, when we thought we could hold onto the business. Every day I saw starving children begging on the street, men in suits doing manual labor for pennies. There are definitely people suffering in cities."

"You had your own place in New York City? I would think you would have stayed at home and gone in to work with your father each day."

Tim looked at the table, now cleared and put to rights. The dirty dishes were stacked next to the sink, below the window where the shadows were growing long. "My wife wanted an apartment in town."

"Your wife?" Carol squeaked out.

Tim saw the panic on her face and took pity on her distress. "Yes, I was married. As soon as I graduated from college I got the job and Theresa convinced me I should have a wife. We married and I bought an apartment and she spent her days furnishing it and going to social gatherings with her friends."

Carol's hand had unconsciously gone to her chin, her fingers delicately covering her mouth, as though to hold back words.

"When the business closed down, Theresa left me. The same day I lost the apartment, she served me with divorce papers. I hear she's in Europe now."

She must have been holding her breath because the whoosh of air escaping was audible. "I'm sorry for your troubles," she whispered.

CHAPTER NINE

s she hurried to a birth, out into the night, Carol had a few minutes to think without distractions. The relief she felt when she realized that Tim was not still married was huge. Not that she was doing anything wrong but her mother always said to avoid even the appearance of sin and if he was married, well, that would be hard to explain. Her, a widow, living there with a married man. Being divorced wasn't anything to be proud of but at least no angry woman was going to show up at the door.

She had let her mother believe that her friend was a woman but after the last letter, she knew she would have to clear that up.

She was pretty sure the neighbors all thought they were married. She didn't try to correct them, or fill them in on what was really going on, mainly because she didn't really know what was going on.

The little house huddled in the dark and Carol tapped twice on the door before quietly turning the knob without waiting for a response. A dog lifted his its head from where it slept on the shadowy living room floor and made a muffled "whoof" sound. A warning or a greeting, she didn't take time to decide. She moved deliberately toward the bedroom at the southwest corner of the room.

Inside, Anna raised her head from where she was resting it upon the wall. She wore a gingham house dress that looked white in the dim room. She grimaced as a greeting before resting her forehead back against the spot on the wall. Her husband sat on the edge of the bed, his hands dangling between his thighs. He wearily registered relief at Carol's arrival and rose, making some nondescript sound accompanied with a gesture that he was stepping out of the room, leaving the two women alone.

Carol put her right hand firmly yet gently

on the laboring woman's back, standing still for
long seconds until the pain that gripped her eased.
"How are you doing?"

"As well as can be expected." And then another contraction held her, dragging her down inside herself.

The moments were counted by the number
of pains. As a glow became noticeable in the window behind the muslin curtains, the power shifted. The low hum of labor became a catching groan,
then a slight grunt until it caught and held and
wrenched the deep sound of hard work. Of push-
ing.

Carol swept the blankets off the bed and
lay down a pad of newspapers enveloped in fabric,
stitched together to protect the bedding.

Anna's fingers tightened on the door frame.
Her face slid down the wall as her knees bent. With
her other hand she reached down, under her dress
and calmly said, "Here it comes."

Quickly, Carol grabbed the newspaper pad
and threw it onto the floor between Anna's feet just
as a gush of liquid splashed down her legs. Carol
dropped to her knees and reached out both hands
to catch the baby as it somersaulted past its moth-

er's hand. Untangling it from the umbilical cord, she passed the naked, wet baby between Anna's legs where it was grasped and brought to its mother's chest to the ecstatic cry, "My baby!"

The door slammed open and there stood the husband, his mouth open, his eyes wide.

Together they helped Anna to the bed.

The woman who had asked Carol to come to her birth a month in the future had delivered a week ago but neither Tim nor Carol brought it up. Every night, dinner was on the table, the garden continued to grow and produce, and the flowers out front bloomed. Tim didn't say she should leave, and she sure wasn't going to volunteer to go.

Every night as the sun dipped behind the mountains to the West, a breeze came up. It wasn't much of a breeze but it felt good and usually they opened the windows to catch it and freshen the house.

The street lights along the avenue out front touched the back yard with only the barest glimmer of light and there was something intimate about sitting on the back stoop with Tim, in the dark, and talking. The radio was low, crackling with a slow love song, and somewhere off in the distance a coyote yipped.

While summer's heat was still oppressive, July's dry air had made way for August monsoons. The dramatic difference from the very subtle and almost nonexistent smell of the desert had metamorphosed into a glorious bouquet of fragrance, made more intense in the damp air. A storm had passed through earlier in the day but now it was clear and the steps had dried.

"This humidity reminds me of being a girl back home. The rains would come in the spring and the whole world seemed to green up and bloom overnight."

"What did you do for fun?" Tim was sitting on the bottom step, his legs stretched out in front of him.

Carol smiled in remembrance. "When I was real little we'd play hide and go seek in the corn field but my mother didn't like us to do that. She was always afraid we'd get so lost we wouldn't be found until harvest." She twitched her skirt back down over her knees and wiggled on the top step to get more comfortable. "Later, when I got older, there were school games and programs and church socials."

"Is that where you met your husband?"

She shook her head. "Mac didn't live too far away and we went to the same school so he was always around." She sighed, and leaned back to look at the stars in the night sky. The swath of the Milky Way was a band of stardust across the heavens. "He was a fun boy and there weren't too many boys, fun or otherwise, so it seemed natural to pair up."

Tim had turned to watch Carol's face. The line of her throat as she gazed skyward, mesmerized him.

"Look!" She sat up straight but still looked up. "A falling star! Make a wish!" She shut her eyes and clenched her fists and her heart spoke what she secretly hoped for: I wish I could stay here with Tim forever.

Tim saw her lips move silently with her secret wish, and then looked up just in time to see another meteor zip by as it burned itself out in

Earth's atmosphere. He would never admit it, because wishing on a falling star seemed childish and silly, but he made a wish anyway.

CHAPTER TEN

*S*ometimes the mailman dropped a letter into the box out front but it didn't happen often. As Carol heard the distinctive sound of the mailbox lid dropping, she wiped her hands on a dish towel and walked to the front door. The heat was stifling today so she was making a huge salad for dinner with fruit for desert. A truck of produce came regularly from California, where ocean breezes kept things growing.

The letter was addressed to her in her mother's handwriting. To savor the pleasure and excitement of receiving mail, she took it back into the kitchen and waited until she had poured a cold glass of lemonade and was sitting at the table, to slice open the flap of the envelope.

Carol's pleasure quickly turned to dismay. Her mother seemed to gloss over Carol's role as midwife. She wrote of the hardship of the dusty winds blowing, the continuing drought, and the lack of help from Washington. The younger children were sickly, the neighbors moving away, and the crops were dying in the fields. But still, Carol's mother insisted, she should return home. She had no business living in Nevada with a man. There were women in Kansas who needed a midwife, too and if that was what Carol was driven to do, she could find births to attend on the dusty prairie.

Carol set the letter down and took a drink of the tartly sweet drink. Was it really so bad that she was there? She'd heard stories about Las Vegas. Prostitutes and Speakeasies on every corner. Unemployed men pouring into the area in hopes of hiring on at the dam and then staying because they had no money to leave. But that was 30 miles away, not here in the Federal Reservation, a planned city with sidewalks and a school and everyone working for pay. She could be doing worse, if she had gone down to the valley. By contrast, Boulder City was a calm oasis of sanity in a country that was suffering. She stood and went to the open window. Her little garden was still struggling in the heat but it was nothing like Kansas, nothing like what her mother described. Trees, sapling really, had been planted along the street. Someday there would be shade and with all that water the dam was providing, there would never be a shortage. The breeze brought some small amount of dust inside but the sun shone brightly, no clouds of blowing dirt to block the light.

She went back to the table, sat and continued reading the letter.

"You must return at once! It is a sin to be living with that man, and your husband not dead a year."

A sin to live here? Or a sin to go back and suffer? She was doing nothing wrong but people couldn't see inside the walls of the house. They didn't know she slept in the porch room or that she and Tim had never so much as kissed. She didn't even know if he found her attractive! She didn't know if he would want her to stay, but she wanted to stay. She wanted to watch the elm trees along the streets grow big and cast shade. She wanted to plant a bigger garden and a patch of lawn. She wanted to see the babies she'd delivered grow into strapping children. And, oh, how she wanted to continue to see Tim each day!

What her mother was saying in the letter was that what Carol wanted didn't matter. The only thing that mattered is what people thought. It didn't matter that the whole country was in a depression, men out of work, Kansas and Oklahoma blowing away. When she should have been proud of her daughter for having found a way to prosper during these bad times, she was only ashamed.

Just a few weeks before, Carol had felt invisible. No one knew her, or missed her, or cared. Her own husband had cared so little he'd dragged her off hundreds of miles away from her family and then up and died, stranding her there. Since she'd started delivering babies, the women in town knew her and children called out a greeting to her on the street. She had a life here and she liked it. What did she have to go back for? Another worker to help support her parents' farm on a dying prairie on the edge of a desolate town? Was that all her mother thought she was good for?

Carol put the letter down and went to her

room. Her pocket book was on the chest of drawers and inside she had a roll of dollar bills, earned honestly at the service of the women of this town. $48, enough to buy a train ticket home.

By the time Tim got home, the salad was waiting, cool and refreshing, and the electric fan had been placed just right to blow on him as he ate. Carol knew how hot it was in Boulder Canyon and she wanted to give him some measure of relief.

"How was your day?" he asked as he dished up salad and fruit onto his plate.

"I got a letter from my mother. She's insisting I go back to Kansas." Carol kept her eyes on her plate.

"Do you want to?" he asked, holding his breath for her answer. She was funny, and kind and had made the little Company house into a home, rough though it might be. He couldn't imagine life without her.

"No. I like it here." she said shortly. She tucked her short hair behind her ears and took another bite of salad.

He breathed a sigh of relief but even as the air whooshed from his lungs he felt guilty for wanting her to stay. He knew she was breaking the law by being on the Reservation and they were both breaking society's law by living together, innocent though they may be of any wrong doing.

He didn't know what this feeling was that he felt for Carol. It wasn't like the firecracker intensity of his initial attraction to his ex-wife. His heart would pound with anticipation of seeing her, he skin felt feverish with desire for her, and she seemed to know it. But, just like a firecracker, his feelings for her had burned out leaving cold ashes in its wake.

What he felt for Carol was more like a gentle fire on a cold night; one that you fed small sticks to keep it going, and held your hands out to warm. He glanced at her face. Her expression was distant as she still worried over her mother's comments.

After dinner, Tim put on a radio program and they sat on the back steps and listened to Jack Benny tease Don Wilson about his weight.

It had been years since Tim had spent any time around a woman. His wife had always smelled of heavy perfume and her hair was carefully arranged; her physical presentation including her expressions and body movements were as artfully contrived. He had learned early in their marriage to not risk disturbing her appearance with an embrace.

By contrast, Carol's hair looked softly mussed and his fingers itched to run through the silky strands. He took a deep breath and absorbed her unembellished unique scent, clean and fresh.

Carol watched him from the corner of her eye. He was looking at her and she felt restless under his gaze. As uncomfortable as it made her feel, she craved more. She leaned toward him as though to a magnet. Risking a glance in his direction their eyes met, and a silent communication passed between them. They had both been married and knew what these these feelings between a man and a woman meant. Carol broke the gaze first. The risk was too great to forget he wasn't really her husband.

The sound of crickets in the garden and out in the desert a coyote yipping, broke the silence when the program ended.

As she stood to turn off the radio, Tim spoke. "Carol," He paused and ran his fingers through his hair. In a voice low, barely heard he said, "If you don't want to leave, don't go. Stay."

"How can I?" She stopped at the top step and turned to him at the bottom, standing on the little board mat she had placed there at the base of the steps in an attempt to catch sand before it made it into the house. Her hand was still on the knob of the radio right inside the back door. "My mother says it's sinful that I'm living here with you. She thinks we're... intimate. Or maybe she just thinks everyone else thinks it. I don't know." She took a deep shuddering breath. "I love it here. I love all of it. All of it." she said intently looking at him.

A weightless feeling hit his belly, rising to his head making him feel almost dizzy. "Then don't go."

"How can I stay, I ask you? Sooner or later the Administration is going to tell me to leave because I'm an unmarried woman without any right to be here. That's if the church-goers in town don't run me out first, according to my mother."

Tim knew that the Admin could make her leave. They were living on borrowed time. In the weeks Carol had been staying with him she hadn't left town once because she was afraid she wouldn't be let back in at the guard gate. "You were married to a worker here and had the right to live within the Reservation."

"Yes," she interrupted, her voice rough with

emotion in a harsh whisper, "but he's dead and I no longer have that right!"

CHAPTER ELEVEN

They lived at the top of Uptown, in a little shanty they had built out of an old dam supply shack. The window in the kitchen overlooked a deep wash, and further a bit of the valley where the Colorado River snaked it's way. At night you could see the lights from the trucks bringing the men home, up the mountain from the dam.

Jane was thirty and some. She and her four surviving children lived in the shanty with her husband, Bill. The rest of her children, those that hadn't survived an outbreak of influenza, were buried back in Missouri.

They were the only black people in town and kept to themselves mostly. The men Bill worked for around town, called him Big Bill because he was tall and barrel chested, with gleaming dark skin and closely cropped black hair. He was imposing and Jane called him William because she felt that was more respectful.

When her pains began late Wednesday night, Big Bill was working the night shift driving a truck back and forth to the dam. She sent Sam, her oldest boy at eleven years old, around the corner to the hospital to tell them her time had come and would they please call William's boss to send him home now. But Sam grew shy and no one paid him any mind in the hospital reception area where everyone seemed busy and important.

He stood in front of the tall desk, hoping for the white lady there to notice him, but she didn't and after awhile he came outside and walked down the way to the sidewalk, not knowing what to do.

Carol was walking back from a delivery, briskly because it was dark and she was ready to be home in bed, listening to Tim's gentle snores from the other room.

The boy was dark and the street was dark so

until he suddenly moved she didn't see him. Startled, she gasped which made him cry out.

In relief, she laughed. "My, you surprised me!" When he looked up at her, and the street light shone on his face, she saw the tracks of tears glistening on his cheeks. "Oh, dear, whatever is wrong?" she asked.

Sam's relief at this kindness was so great his voice came out in a sob. "My mom is having the baby and I don't know what to do."

"Take me to her," Carol said and as he turned back toward the edge of the desert at the top of Uptown, she followed.

A lamp burned in the window but barely made a dent in the gloom. When Sam opened the door she followed right behind him.

The tidy little home was crowded with furniture and dimly lit. A bed held the bumps of three small bodies, sleeping deeply by the sound of their heavy slow breaths. The slight, lingering scent of bacon grease and something else, something spicy, hung in the air. A cat curled up between the sleeping children, raised its head in curiosity and then went back to sleep. At the end of the room was a doorway, a lighter rectangle in the darkness.

Jane was in her rocking chair, the same chair that had gotten her through the seemingly endless nights of nursing babies and soothing teething pains, but her movements were slight as she concentrated on the tightening of her belly, the stretching of her inner parts. So engrossed in her sensations, she didn't notice them until Sam had whispered "Mama" several times. Her face registered her surprise at the white girl standing just inside the bedroom door.

"I couldn't get anyone at the hospital to listen to me, Mama." He began to cry again at failing her.

Carol stepped forward. "Ma'am, I've been helping the ladies in town and if you like, I'll help you."

Hours later, Big Bill took off his shoes outside the kitchen door and stepped inside in his stocking feet. It was almost dawn and it had been a long night. He wanted something to eat and then sleep but a noise from the other room stopped him. He stood still as a stone, his head cocked to one side like a dog does, listening.

The low murmur of a woman's voice could be heard but it didn't sound like Jane. Then a groan, low but deep and guttural. His heart sped up as he quickly looked around him for a weapon with which to protect his family. His hand found a cast iron frying pan sitting clean and ready on a cold burner of the stove. As he lifted it his eyes never moved from the direction of that curious sound.

He had taken one silent step toward the doorway, toward the sound, when suddenly a cry. Unmistakably a baby's cry. Bill later couldn't recall taking the steps into the bedroom, but suddenly there he was, standing at the end of the bed, looking down upon his wife.

Jane's nightgown was rucked up and a fresh, wet baby lay on her chest. A glistening, shining, coiled cord, all purply grey still attached the baby to something hidden below. A white lady, not more than a girl really, was sitting on the edge of the bed smiling and as she turned to him her smile widened.

Carol saw the man, she assumed Jane's husband, standing there looking stunned. In his hand was an enormous frying pan.

"William, our baby is here. Come see our baby," Jane cried out in joy.

"How'd this happen? I thought you were

going over to the hospital to telephone. We had it planned; they were going to call me."

"Never mind that now. Come, see our baby."

As he tiptoed to her side, his demeanor softened. His shock and fear were draining away leaving the wonder of birth in it's place. "Well, well, what sort of baby did we get?"

"Why, I never looked." Jane laughed and peeked down at the baby, moving a tiny leg out of the way to better see. "A boy! Oh, William, we have another boy," she cried as though it were the most brilliant thing that had ever happened.

Carol woke late, the two births of the day and night before having worn her out. She stretched in her bed and then stilled, listening for sounds that Tim was still at home. No sounds came to her except birds twittering in the small tree out along the street.

After a full bath and clean clothes, she made herself toast slathered with strawberry jam. The dollars earned yesterday were already tucked away in her pocket book but she took out the memories of Jane's birth to savor as she ate.

The children's delight when they woke to meet their new baby brother had been fun to see and William's giant hands cradling the tiny baby had brought tears to her eyes.

Eventually she tidied her toast crumbs and stepped out the back door to check on her garden. It had been neglected yesterday and in the heat of summer, she feared one day might have been enough to kill the plants.

To her great delight, other than a slight wilting of the tender lettuce, all the plants had weathered her absence. She bent to fill the bucket with water from the spigot.

"Carol!" Mary called from her own backyard, next door, even as she began hurrying over.

"Good morning." Carol smiled broadly, still feeling the miracle of the birth room.

Mary's face was pinched in concern. "Were you at Mrs. Jennings' delivery yesterday?"

"Yes, I was. She had a girl and named her Sarah."

"Oh, good," Mary said in relief. "I knew there was some misunderstanding."

Carol's brow wrinkled in confusion. "What misunderstanding? What are you talking about?"

"I was at the grocery this morning and Mrs. Thom said you attended that negro woman's birth last night."

"You mean Jane Crocker? Yes, I did, after the Jennings were settled. Why?"

"I don't know if that was such a good idea. Does your husband know?"

Carol's confusion deepened. "No, he was asleep when I got home and gone when I woke. Whatever could be the problem? I left them at dawn and they were fine. Did something happen to them?"

"Some people might have a problem with it is all. You know, her being black and you being white. I'm sure it will work out."

But it didn't. By evening Mary had heard more gossip, whispered over the mailboxes and at the street corner and on front porch steps.

Tim sent word he would be working through the night. Carol wished he were home so she could tell him what was being said, all the things being reported back to her by Mary. A lady living on California Street, no one Carol knew, was up in arms. According to Mary, this lady was saying to anyone that would listen, that something wasn't right when an engineer's wife was resorting to delivering negro babies. She was threatening to go to Sims Ely about it, to get to the bottom of it.

At dusk Mary had met Carol by the flower patch out front and updated her. "This could jeopardize your husband's job, Carol. Mr. Ely is the ruler of this town and if he doesn't like something, it ends."

After all that Tim had done for her, she couldn't let him suffer the backlash. If Ely found out they weren't married and had been living together, Tim could lose his job. Everything he had worked for would be lost. She didn't dare think of what could happen to her.

CHAPTER TWELVE

*S*he paced back and forth in the dark silent house until her decision was made. Quickly, before she lost courage and could change her mind with false hope, she packed up the barest of essentials in one string bag. She carefully tucked the roll of dollar bills into a folded handkerchief which she pinned to her petticoat under her dress. She would have Tim send her the rest of her things once this had all blown over and she was settled elsewhere. Then she stepped outside.

The dark streets seemed less friendly than they did when she was going to or returning from a birth. She tried to keep to shadows as she silently made her way toward the gatehouse that guarded the entrance to Boulder City. It wouldn't do to get caught after curfew in the government controlled town.

It was very late by the time she made it to the guard shack. A man was inside the small wooden building. He was sitting on a metal office chair, tipped back on two legs, reading a dime novel under the bright glare of a bare light bulb that hung from the ceiling. He licked his finger and turned a page, eyes never leaving the book.

Carol hesitated in the dark, watching him from the edge of the road. Satisfied he was thoroughly engrossed in the book she walked briskly through the gate toward Railroad Pass.

No headlights pierced the night for a long while but soon her eyes became adjusted to the darkness of the desert. Above, the Milky Way could be seen as a band of stars and brighter glow across the sky.

The Railroad Pass community was rough and she had no desire to meet up with anyone there. A casino and tent city, complete with prostitutes, gambling and hard liquor, nestled in the cradle between two mountains, the pass was a dangerous place to stop. Carol knew she couldn't climb over the mountains to avoid the area but she would do her best to pass through unnoticed. She cut back to the right, behind the casino building and in the shadow of the mountain, but because her eyes were used to darkness, she found her way.

Surely it was nearing dawn, she thought, but there wasn't enough moonlight to see her watch pinned to her blouse.

Her feet were sore and grooves had formed in her fingers from holding the string bag, no matter that she switched hands frequently.

Reaching the crest of the hill, once safely beyond the Railroad Pass tent city, she paused, looking out over the valley. In the distance a cluster of twinkling lights indicated the town of Las Vegas. About the same population as Boulder City, it boasted 5000 inhabitants, but where Boulder City, under the iron control of Sims Ely, prohibited spirits, gambling and immoral behavior, in Las Vegas it seemed that anything goes.

As she walked downhill toward the lights, along the side of the road now, a fearful excitement stirred in her chest. She had heard such stories of immorality and lawlessness about the little town ahead, she almost lost her nerve and turned around. But she didn't, marching forward as though to her death, terrified, and exhausted. The stories were frightful, but this was her sacrifice to protect Tim.

Forcefully she reminded herself of Tim's kindness to her, the generosity he had shown when she had nowhere to go and no hope to go on. Taking a deep breath, she stepped forward, one foot at a time toward an uncertain fate.

As she walked memories came unbidden to her mind. The safe feeling she had when she stood next to Tim, so tall and quietly strong. The scent of his skin, heated from the sun, like baking bread. How her heart beat faster when his fingers grazed hers as they passed a dish across the table during dinner. The nights she lay in bed listening to his deep sleeping breaths, wishing she could curl into his arms, feeling her blood coursing through her veins and heat pooling in her belly, needing him as much as she needed air to breathe. Her courage carried her forward and her sacrifice gave her strength.

A light from behind was approaching rapidly causing her shadow to stretch out before her. She stepped quickly off the pavement, into the rocky desert but not soon enough to avoid being seen.

The car came to a stop and then crawled along next to Carol, keeping pace with her stride. She could see there were four men inside, two in front and two in back. They wore white shirts but she couldn't see any more than that.

The man nearest Carol, sitting on the passenger side in the front seat, leaned out the open window. "Ma'am," he said by way of greeting. "How do you do?"

"I am fine, thank you. Good evening." She spoke in as brave a voice as she could muster. Stories of women mistreated by rough men were recalled in an instant and she felt her legs tremble in fear.

"Would you like a ride someplace?" he asked.

Carol considered his question. She surely couldn't outrun these men if they were inclined to attack her. She also knew it would take her many more hours to reach the edges of the town before her. Taking a gamble, she made a split second decision. She agreed that she would like a ride and quickly was tucked between the two men in the

roomy back seat, bag on her lap, skirt pulled de-
murely over her knees, as the car sped down the
hill into the Las Vegas valley.

"Aren't you the midwife?" the driver asked.

"Yes."

"Where you going in the middle of the
night? Is someone having a baby in Las Vegas?"

Carol seized on this explanation. "Yes, one
of my Mormon ladies."

"I know that neighborhood. We can drop
you right off."

The boarding house wasn't bad. It was clean
and the food was plentiful. The couple running the
house were Mormons and had heard of her work in
the next town over.

"You'll find some ladies in need of your services here," the woman, Mrs. Gubler said. "We do
have a midwife but she's often quite busy." Before
long Carol was learning the streets of downtown as
she attended to women.

CHAPTER THIRTEEN

Tim came home to a silent house each evening. He ate at the commissary some nights and some nights he opened a tin of meat or stew to tide him over.

He missed her. It seemed he had never lived alone until now, and now he didn't know how.

He had learned from Mrs. Keith next door, what had happened and though he could surmise why Carol had left he felt she should have talked with him and together they could have weathered the gossip.

Days passed. Monsoon season left and the fluffy clouds of Autumn sailed overhead. He watered Carol's gardens faithfully but couldn't bring himself to find pleasure in the tomatoes she would never slice or the flowers she would never arrange in a vase.

One morning as he sat at the kitchen table, wearing an undershirt and unbelted pants, unshaven, uncombed, looking and feeling sorry for himself, he idly ate a boiled egg and listened halfheartedly to the radio broadcast news.

It was a rare day off for him, a Sunday, and the late September sunshine poured in the window at the front door. A shadow cut off the sunshine followed by a weak knock at the door.

Through the window of the door Tim saw a half-grown boy, maybe 14 or 15 standing there holding the hand of a little girl about five. Both were dressed in their Sunday best, hair slicked back with a wet comb and cheeks still red from scrubbing breakfast away.

Tim's heart sank and he considered not opening the door. He was sure they were calling for the services of a midwife and he would have to tell them she no longer lived there. But, he reasoned, as he opened the door, it was better to tell them so that their mother could make other arrangements.

The boy stammered in embarrassment to speak of the private business of women and birthing. His cheeks grew even redder, flushed with heat. "My ma wanted me to give this to the midwife." He thrust a package, a bundle of cloth, into Tim's hands.

"What's this?" he asked.

"My Aunt Betty had her baby last week and Ma wants the midwife to give this stuff to her. She said to tell her that Ma will come visit next week."

Tim saw that this was a bundle of baby things; clothes and nappies wrapped up in a baby blanket tied at the corners. "Where does your Aunt Betty live?"

Tim took the time to bathe, shave and dress in a suit and tie. He combed his hair back from his face as he stuffed the last bit of boiled egg in his mouth and headed out the door with the bundle of baby things for Aunt Betty.

Outside he paused. The air was fresh, and clouds skidded across the sky, too high to interfere with the bright sunshine. The flower bed seemed to glow in the light; red, orange, yellow and white flowers spilled over the rock boundary Carol had arranged to keep the soil in place. On impulse, he plucked a marigold, the stem easily breaking, and brought it along.

Everyone knew where the Mormon Church was, Mormon or not. The boy had said his aunt lived near the church so that was where Tim headed. Gathered around the train station and courthouse, the streets were lined with tidy houses and shady trees. Grass and flowers graced nearly every yard and the scent of yesterday's mowing still hung heavy over the neighborhood.

He pulled his car up to the little chapel. No cross graced the spire and the sign in front identified it as the Church of Jesus Christ of Latter Day Saints. Families stood about on the lawn and steps and near parked cars, talking amongst themselves. Occasional laughter rang out, while the children tried to stand by obediently but were sometimes overcome with a fit of giggles.

"Excuse me," he called out to one family,

the mother holding a newly born baby. "I'm looking for a midwife. Her name is Carol."

Following the directions he'd been given, Tim drove a few streets over to where a large stone house stood. A placard was propped up in the window saying there were rooms to let, and to inquire within. He grabbed the half-wilted marigold and the bundle from the front seat of the car and walked toward the front door. Pausing, he tried to formulate what he would say but before he could form a coherent thought, the door opened and there was Carol.

Carol couldn't believe her eyes. Tim stood before her looking like he was on his way to one of the important meetings he attended at the Dam. His hair was combed back from his broad forehead, and his tie was still in a tight knot at his neck. A little dab of blood on his neck indicated he was freshly shaved. Shade from the big elm trees on either side of the walk put his face in shadow and hid his expression.

"Can we talk?" he asked. She nodded and crossed her arms.

They walked silently to a park around the corner where they stopped. "Here. This is for you."

He thrust the flower toward her. "From your garden."

"Thank you," she replied quietly. Why was he here? Had the news finally gotten back to Mr. Ely and Tim had lost his job? Surely the fact that she was gone would serve in his favor. "Why are you here? Did you get fired?"

He shook his head. "No, no. Nothing like that."

"Remember our conversation one night? You said you would have a right to be on the Reservation if you were a worker's wife. And you said, that since your husband was dead, you were no longer married to a worker. But if you were married to a worker you could stay. Your mother's argument that you were being sinful wouldn't be valid, either."

Carol looked at him, standing there in the shadow of the park. A cool breeze came up out of nowhere and brushed across her cheeks and it was only then that she realized she was crying,

"I'm a worker. If you were my wife you could come back to Boulder City."

"Don't tease me, Tim!" She squeezed her hands together and brought them to her chin. "Are you asking me to marry you?" She held her breath for his answer.

"Yes," he cleared his throat. "I am. Carol, will you marry me?"

Her tears flowed freely now and dried almost as fast as she shed them in the Autumn breeze. "If you mean it, then yes. Yes."

Tim closed the distance between them with one stretch of his legs and put his arms around her. He held her as she cried and then, when the tears slowed, he tilted her head back and kissed her soft lips. "By the way," he whispered against her cheek, "Our new house is ready for us to move into."

CHAPTER FOURTEEN

The muffled bell of the phone woke her in the early dawn. She kept a pillow over it at night to try to quiet it some for Tim's sake, but it always woke her up. Quickly she dressed and grabbed the small valise she used. Inside were the instruments she'd managed to acquire and some herbal remedies as well as a change of clothing. She tried to be quiet because Tim was sleeping still, one of his few days off, but just as she was opening the front door of their stucco house in the engineer's neighborhood, he came out of the bedroom, his hair sticking up in all directions, pajama pants hanging low on his slim hips.

"Mrs. Sutherland over on G?" he asked.

Carol nodded. "I'm surprised you didn't hear the telephone."

Tim wrapped his arms around her and rested his chin on the crown of her head. "No, I seldom hear it." He paused. "That new doctor will be at the hospital soon. You'll be out of a job."

"That'll be fine," she said with a wistful smile. "I'll be busy with other things."

They stood in the open doorway, looking out over the green lawn that sloped away from their home. Carol breathed deeply of the morning air, redolent with the scent of grass, and creosote, and roses. Winter had been brief and here it was Spring again. The sky was lightening by the minute and soon she would have to rush off down the hill, down to the Six Company houses where a woman waited for her but for just a second she leaned into her husband.

Tim was watching the sky, growing lighter, speeding toward the day, enough to illuminate the few high clouds moving over the valley. The saplings planted in the parkways between the streets and the sidewalks glowed with the fresh green of new leaves, lending an aura of life over the streets of the avenues below them. He turned Carol in his arms so that she was leaning back against his chest and he brought his hands around to cradle her growing belly. Their baby, a miracle, in so many ways.

"I love you," he whispered against her hair.

"And I love you back," she said and he could hear the smile in her voice. Then, suddenly she was gone, waving goodbye with a grin, as she strode off down the hill toward Avenue G and a new beginning.